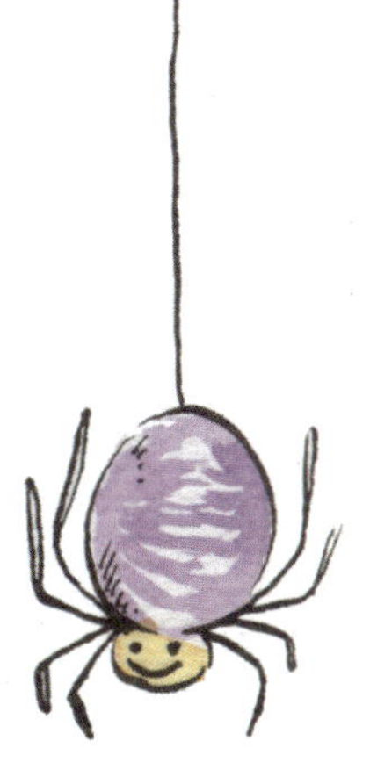

This book belongs to:

The Not So Wise Owl

Author: Robert James Parfett

Illustrated by: Sarah-Leigh Wills

Graphics: Simon Hopkins

Dedication: To my Rachel, William and Oliver for your support and inspiration, RJP

ISBN: 978-0-9560331-6-1

ChildrensStoryPublishers.com

Tel: 0845 475 3625   Post: Tipyn O Gymru, Tewkesbury, GL20 8HA United Kingdom

The Not So
Wise Owl
Illustrations
Sarah-Leigh Wills
Author
Robert James Parfett

In a gnarly old oak sat a tatty old owl

With his popping out eyes and his permanent scowl.

And no twitting or twooing could ever be heard

Not a snippet of wisdom nor a sensible word.

Though the other oak dwellers at first couldn't see

What was wrong with the funny old owl in the tree.

A squirrel was first to arrive on the scene.

He stared at the owl who looked terribly mean.

"Good morning Owl! Could I just have a word?

You are a wise and intelligent bird.

I have a dilemma; I don't have a clue

Where my acorns have gone, I was hoping you do!"

Owl turned his head with a curious grin

"A packet of crisps then turn left in Berlin!

Red sky at night and some Turkish Delight.

Pass me the butter! Those fleas want to bite!"

Squirrel was speechless and scurried away.

"Owl must be having a difficult day!"

A woodpecker flew up to where Owl still swayed.

Approaching quite slowly and looking afraid.

"Good morning Owl! Could I just have a word?

You are a wise and intelligent bird.

I have a dilemma; I can't seem to make

Any holes with my beak and it keeps me awake."

Owl flapped his wings and looked up at the sky.

"When will we meet again? Hot apple pie!

Wash it in vinegar, head for the moon!

The pig with the ring has the runcible spoon!"

Woodpecker, startled, flew down from the tree.

"Poor Owl is so confused. He's all at sea!"

A spider climbed slowly up onto Owl's head

"I want him to hear me!" The small creature said.

"Good morning Owl! Could I just have a word?

You are a wise and intelligent bird.

I have a dilemma; my webs always break!

I've been up all night and my legs really ache!"

Owl's eyes grew wide then he started to sing.

"Elephants only play jazz in the spring!
Rotten flamingos drink ketchup and squeak.
My Auntie Matilda just married a leek!"

Spider climbed rapidly down to the floor.

"Owl doesn't seem to be there anymore!"

A meeting was called at the foot of the oak
And there gathered all of the tree's little folk.
To talk about Owl and discuss what to do.
"Where has the Owl gone that we all once knew?
He doesn't make sense! He can't utter a word
Without saying something bizarre or absurd."

"Look!" cried a robin, "He's fallen asleep!"

Owl started leaning then fell in a heap.

"Don't owls go out at night? That's his mistake!

Why's he not hunting? He should be awake!"

"Of course!" cried the others, "There is no way

He should be so busy during the day!"

All of the animals waited to see

If Owl's lack of sleep really could be the key!

They tried and they tried to wake Owl from his snooze

Eager to tell him the wonderful news.

"Owl you're not loopy. Don't give up the fight.

You are nocturnal, try hunting at night!"

Owl seemed to twitch and he lifted his head
"I always knew it was not time for bed!
All of your questions at every hour
Took all my wisdom and sapped all my power.
So when the sun shines please, leave me alone.
No pestering creatures! A question free zone!"

That night the oak dwellers went to see Owl

Who no longer had his ridiculous scowl.

"Good evening Owl, could we just have a word?"

Twitting and twooing and laughter were heard.

Creatures from far and wide all came to see

The jolly wise owl in the gnarly old tree.